by

Tony Varrato

LIBRARY AND ARCHIVES CANADA CATALOGUING IN PUBLICATION

Varrato, Tony, 1966–
    Outrage / Tony Varrato.

(HIP edge)
ISBN 978-1-897039-28-1

I. Title. II. Series.

PZ7.V378Ou 2008   j813'.6   C2007-906952-5

General editor: Paul Kropp
Text design: Laura Brady
Illustrations drawn by: Catherine Doherty
Cover design: Robert Corrigan

1 2 3 4 5 6 7   08 07 06 05 04 03

Printed and bound in Canada

High Interest Publishing acknowledges the financial support of the
Government of Canada through the Book Publishing Industry
Development Program (BPIDP) for our publishing activities.

Connor's had a rough day — punched out by a buddy, kicked out of school, beaten up on the way home. And then he gets accused of robbing a corner store. It all sucks, big time.

CHAPTER ONE

Some Days Just Suck

I was so angry, my hands shook. I wanted to punch somebody. I *needed* to punch somebody. It had been that kind of day.

I pedaled my bike as fast as I could. At least I got out of the pizza shop before I slugged Ken, my manager. The guy had smiled at me! He had smiled and twirled a pizza when he told me to go home. "Get out of here, Connor. You get tossed out of school, don't even think about coming to work."

Just what I needed. It would have felt good to

smash his face with that pizza. But I'd lose my job for sure. And I needed the money if I was going to get some real wheels. Imagine, me, seventeen and still riding a crummy bike.

My hands shook the handlebars. I was looking for a fight. Or maybe I was looking to finish the fight that started at school. I was going to find that fight if I had to pedal all over town.

I sped down Canal Street, past the factory, half hoping Dad might be outside to see me. That would show him. "Hey!" I screamed in my head, "I *am* the screwed-up punk you always say I am!" But there was no one there, no one to really scream at.

I turned south on Canal Street. This road went past the boxing club. Maybe someone there would want to duke it out. And the police station. Maybe they'd hassle me for not being in school. I'd just tell them, "Ha! I've been tossed out of school. So bug off!"

I pedaled faster.

I could feel the sweat on my chest and the burn

in my legs. This was good. The sweat and pain made me feel a little better. They made my hands shake less. They cleared my head a little.

The screw-up started first thing. I was just walking to second period when Shawn came up to me. The guy has a mouth, but most days he knows when to stop. Not today. I've known Shawn since elementary school. A few years back, we'd played baseball together. Shawn could really throw a baseball. And we were friends, kind of. Maybe we're still friends, but today he crossed the line. He dissed my mom. *Nobody* disses my mom, ever! So I slugged him, right in the mouth.

I'm quick, but Shawn has a few pounds on me. He called me a "red-haired freak," and nailed my left eye. I think the guy hit my new brow-piercing on purpose.

That stings, big time.

So the fight got ugly fast. We slammed each other

into the lockers. We pounded each other as hard as we could . . . for about one minute.

Old Mr. Donkas broke us up and dragged us into the office. Now we're both out of school for ten days. And when I tried to do something right with my time off, Ken shoved it back down my throat. And he smiled. He *smiled*! It wasn't fair. It never was.

I almost turned right on Bendigo to head back home. Almost.

I needed to pedal a little longer. I needed to burn off that last bit of anger. I was nearly beat from pedaling as fast as I could. I didn't want to go home until I had to crawl. Then I'd collapse on the couch and sleep. That's what I needed.

I knew I was wearing out. My tired muscles didn't feel too good. I decided I wasn't looking for a fight anymore.

And wouldn't you know, that's exactly when I found it.

I was pumping my pedals down Canal Street for

all I was worth and drove by the nightclub. It was one o'clock, so it was deserted this time of day. Even the staff didn't get there until about four.

But as I passed the empty parking lot, I saw a familiar bike parked at the side. Glancing back, I saw Shawn throwing rocks at the side of a building. I guess he wasn't trying to bust any windows because none of them were broken. Just passing the time.

I slowed down a little to watch him, and he looked my way. I flipped him off to say thanks for the swollen eye a few hours ago. He signaled back with one of the rocks in his hand. He hit me in the back. It didn't really hurt too bad, but I could tell he had tossed it with all his might. He had pretty good aim; that was a heck of a throw. But his marksmanship wasn't going to save him from another clobbering.

I hit the brakes to skid my back tires around. I half expected him to hit me with another rock. But he was just standing there daring me to come over.

I hate to be dared.

I pedaled across the grass and the parking lot. I leapt off my bike before it fell onto its side. I moved fast. I was in his face in no time.

He didn't back away. "I don't need this today, Connor!"

"You think I do?" I yelled back. "I got suspended, and I've got to get my brow re-pierced."

"You shoulda thought about that before you hit me!" We were so close, Shawn was spitting on me. "You take another swing at me, and I'll knock that red dye right out of your hair."

"You talked about my mom!" I spit back. "If you dis my mom . . ."

"Hey, the truth ain't a dis!" Shaw shouted. "She's been with half the town, Connor. So she's a . . ."

I shoved him. "Shut up!"

"Or what?" He shoved back. "I'll punch your right eye so you match?"

"Bring it on!" I shoved him again. "There's no teacher to save your sorry butt now."

In fact, there was no one around at all. It was just the two of us. We could pound each other, and no one would witness it. We wouldn't get into trouble. No one could stop us until one of us was lying unconscious on the asphalt.

I don't even remember who slugged who first. I do remember him hitting the piercing rod in my right eyebrow and sending a shot of pain through the whole right side of my face. I could feel the pain in my eye down to my jaw. I was sure he was aiming for that spot all along.

I slugged him fast. My arms were dishing out three punches for each one of his. But I figured we were about even because each of his jabs had a lot more power. I ducked and blocked quite a few. Even so, there was no place on my head or chest that didn't hurt.

After what seemed like an hour, but must have been just a few minutes, we stood facing each other. His lip was swollen and bloody. I wondered if I had knocked out a tooth. My right eye was nearly as swollen as my left and I could see only through slits. It was like wearing a cheap Halloween mask with the eye holes cut too small.

Our arms were so tired the punches were weak, and we were just going through the motions. There wasn't even any pain on impact, just dull thuds as we hit each other. We slugged at each other until we both fell down, beaten and exhausted. Neither of us won the fight.

We probably laid there for fifteen minutes. There was no way I had the strength to raise my arms and check my watch. I could hear Shawn panting near me, but I didn't feel like looking over to see exactly where he collapsed.

And then I started to notice a chunk of asphalt digging into the back of my head. It dawned on me that I had no way to leave here gracefully. I couldn't stand up and yell, *This isn't over!* Because it was. I couldn't grab my bike and ride off, flipping Shawn the bird. The truth was, I didn't think I could move my arms anymore.

I was going to have to limp to my bike and hobble home like a dog with his tail between his legs. Or I could just lay here until four o'clock when the staff would get here and call the police.

I figured it was better to hobble like a dog.

I got up to find that Shawn was already up and limping to his bike. We didn't speak. I wasn't mad at him anymore, but I wasn't even sure I was in the first place. Either way, I certainly didn't want to talk to him right now. I might say something stupid like *I'm sorry* or *Friends shouldn't fight*. That was just too corny.

Shawn headed north on Canal, so I decided to go south. There was a corner store just down the road. I thought I'd go there and get a frozen Coke. First to put on my swollen eyes, and then to drink. The store clerk might not like my face too much. I looked like road kill, but I didn't care.

It wasn't like I was going to rob the place.

CHAPTER TWO

The Robbery

My legs were shot even before the short ride to the corner store. The swelling around my eyes made it hard to see the road well, but Canal Street wasn't busy this time of day. I must have hit every pothole there was. Each pothole sent a lightning bolt of pain from my stomach and chest right up to my head.

This old corner store was one of the few that hadn't been bought out by a big chain. It must have had a name once. Now, there was just a broken sign that said "Gas."

After I parked, I chained up my bike to the rack. The pain in my fingers made it take five times longer than normal to work the lock and wrap the cord. For the first time, I noticed my knuckles were swollen and bloody.

I heard a thump, thump, thump, thump from a car that pulled in behind me. Techno, with a heavy beat. I didn't look at the car; it hurt too much to turn my head. But I noticed the driver never turned off the engine. The guy didn't get out, either. I guessed he got a look at my face and decided to wait until after I left. I didn't blame him.

Thump, thump, thump, thump! I didn't know the song, but it had the same beat as my throbbing head.

With swollen, bloody hands, I pulled the door open and walked in. The store was quiet except for the ding when I entered. When I walked past the potato chip rack, I saw the old man who worked there. And he saw me.

Old Riley was one of those guys everybody recognized. He'd been working behind that counter forever. I wasn't sure if Riley was his first name or his last. His face said he was somewhere between seventy and a hundred and seventy, but that tough old guy looked like he could kick some butt. He sure could kick mine right about now.

Riley was filling up the cigarette display behind the counter. He stopped with a carton of smokes still in his hand. I guess he took a look at me and was trying to decide. Should he call the cops or an ambulance?

"Hey, Riley," I mumbled. "It's okay, man." My sore jaw wasn't going to let me say much more. I was trying to let him know I was just here to buy something. There was no need to get out the pepper spray or anything.

I went down the snack aisle and briefly thought about getting a bag of chips. The bag I had for lunch was long gone and my tank was empty. However, just the thought of chewing something made my mouth hurt. I decided to get the frozen Coke and just slurp that until I got home.

I picked the extra large cup and filled it up with the stuff. I grabbed a dome lid and with a little effort I snapped it closed. I had more trouble with the straws. My swollen fingers weren't doing so good with picking up small stuff. I must have dropped about a dozen on the floor. I bent over and had to scoop them up with both hands acting like a clamp.

Then I heard the ding of the door.

I got the straws off the floor, but there was no way they were going back in the little cup. So I dropped them on the counter. *Sorry about that, Riley*, I thought.

I looked toward the counter. The old man was still staring at me. I walked over to the counter, holding the drink between both my nearly useless hands.

I put the drink on the counter and tried to flash Riley a grin. I figured I'd show him my charming side. I had a hunch Riley still wanted to pick up the phone or the pepper spray.

I looked toward the parking lot and saw the car was now empty, but I could hear the thump of the bass. Either the driver had left it on or my head was getting ready to explode.

I reached my right hand into my pocket to get out some money. That's when somebody pushed me. Hard.

I fell toward the counter and bumped my drink. I lurched to catch it before it fell behind and splattered all over the floor.

Maybe it was the hands; maybe it was my messed-up brain. But I didn't make it. The drink went all over the floor. *Sorry again, Riley.*

Riley jumped back to get out of the way while I was half sprawled on the counter. And then it all happened, in no time.

A guy came around the counter and hit the old man with a club. Once, twice, and then he stopped. Riley fell to the floor. Then the guy grabbed the bills from the open cash register and headed toward the front door.

I froze for a second. I was still leaning across the counter, feeling stupid. What to do? Help Riley or chase the bad guy?

Easy choice. I was already mad. And the guy had hit an old man.

So I went after the punk. I sprinted with more energy than I thought I had. I got out the door, but the punk had a head start and a running car. All I could do was stand there, wave my arms and yell.

The car was gone.

Did I think to look at the license plate? Of course not. That was one of those things that you yell at the screen when you're watching a hold-up on TV. "Hey, idiot! Get the license plate number!"

Well, I was that idiot. I didn't get the number. I just watched as the dark green car tore down Canal Street. Then I went back in the store to see about Riley.

I walked over to the old man leaning against the

wall. Blood was dripping down his head on one side. A big bruise was on the other. Riley wasn't standing too well.

But he was standing well enough to hold a phone. "Yeah, I've got one of 'em right here," he said into the phone.

I wanted to say that I wasn't *one of 'em*. But the baseball bat he clutched in his other hand told me to keep my swollen mouth shut.

The sirens were already getting close.

CHAPTER THREE

I Protest

When the cops arrived, I protested.

Believe me, I protested.

From the minute the cars rolled up with their lights flashing and sirens wailing, I protested. Even before the police were out of their cars, I protested.

They drew their weapons.

I protested, though my aching jaw and fat lips weren't cooperating. "Hey, you've got the wrong guy."

"Kneel down!"

"You've got the wrong guy," I said louder, but I followed directions well.

"Put your hands up!"

They barked a whole bunch of other things while they checked me for weapons. Then they cuffed me. One cop started lecturing me about something, but I tuned him out. This whole thing was too stupid.

The other cop was inside the store, talking to Riley. The old man had put down the bat and was lying on the floor again. He didn't look too good.

"You've got the wrong guy," I told them. I knew I sounded stupid, but I couldn't think of anything else to say. I didn't do it. What else was there to tell them?

I yelled in pain when the cop pulled me to my feet. My shoulders hurt bad.

I fit in one more, "You've got the wrong guy," before the policeman held my head and pushed me into the back of the car. I wondered if he really wanted to hit me against the car once for fun, just before he threw me in the back.

He slammed the door and went inside with his partner.

Alone, I stared through the metal grate at the store. How does stuff like this happen? How could I start the day sitting in math class this morning and end up sitting in a police car? Some days, a guy shouldn't get out of bed.

I stared out the window and into the store as much as possible. One cop was talking into a radio and scanning the store. The other was looking at Riley's head.

An ambulance pulled in. Two guys grabbed the stretcher and wheeled it inside.

I went numb for a few minutes. I watched the ambulance guys and policemen move around and do their things. And somewhere in my brain I kept thinking that they were going to try to pin this all on me.

They wheeled Riley out right past my window. He looked bad. They had an oxygen mask on him and a bandage on his head. I could see a lot of blood on his clothing.

Why did he call the cops on me? Why did he pick up the bat? There was no way he could think I hit him! No way he could think I robbed him!

I tried to convince myself that this was no big deal. These cops were smart. They were paid to solve crimes. They could figure out that it wasn't me, couldn't they?

The ambulance pulled away, and I hoped the old guy would be all right. For his sake as well as mine.

One officer came back and sat in the front seat. Maybe it was my fuzzy vision, but I noticed his lips stuck off his face kind of like a chicken's beak. I decided not to tell him. I figured he already knew, and he wouldn't want me to remind him.

Chicken Lips put something on the seat next to him, but I couldn't see what.

Suddenly, I thought of something new to say. "I'm innocent."

Chicken Lips said nothing and started the car.

Maybe he hadn't heard me. Maybe his brain

didn't work right. So I slowed it down for him. "I . . . didn't . . . do . . . anything."

He lifted up the object that he had thrown on the seat next to him. It was an old-style video cassette. "This tape says you did."

He drove off, and neither of us said another word.

The seats in the police station were way less comfortable than the seats in the principal's office. Having my hands cuffed didn't help either.

Chicken Lips was busy typing at a computer. The guy could really type. I figured since he was part chicken, maybe all he was good at was pecking those keys. I smiled a little. Sometimes I crack myself up.

"Something funny?"

"Uh, no."

"You sure? I like a good laugh." From the look on his face, I don't think he had laughed in the last decade.

"Look, I had nothing to do with robbing that store."

"Save it," the guy said and looked back at his computer screen. "Name?"

"Connor Mullins."

"Age?"

"Seventeen."

We went through that whole deal. I was finger-printed on a computer. That was kind of interesting because I didn't have to get ink all over my hand. Then the cops took my picture. They took out the rod in my eyebrow, maybe so I'd look pretty. One cop gave me a napkin with ice inside for my face.

Chicken Lips stuck me in a holding cell with another guy. I lay down on the bench and put the ice pack on my eyes.

"What'd you do?" the other guy asked.

Was he talking to me? I didn't care. I was too tired.

"Hey!" This time his voice was a little louder.

I lifted up the ice pack and turned my head to see

a skinny guy about ten feet from me. He was maybe 18, dressed in ripped jeans and a flannel shirt. He was lying back on the other bench. He looked bored.

"What'd you do?" he repeated like he was in a hurry or something.

I put the ice back on my face. "I didn't do nothin'."

He grunted. "Yeah, you look like you didn't do nothin'." He grunted again just in case I missed his sarcasm. "I'm guessin' that you fought a couple of cops," he said. "Or maybe just one cop who really didn't like you too much."

I kept the ice on my face. Was this guy trying to yank my chain? Was he looking for a fight? Well, he wasn't going to get one. This hard wooden bench felt like the most comfortable place I'd been for hours. There wasn't much that could make me move right then.

"All I did was try to buy a frozen Coke, and they arrested me for robbing a store."

"Ha!" It was a loud, rude laugh. "Look, man, I'm not a cop or a lawyer. I'm just trying to pass some time. I've been here about seven hours now, and I just want to talk. If you want to be a jerk and not talk to me, then okay , whatever! But don't give me a load of garbage like I'm an idiot! You don't get a face like that and a ripped shirt just by buying a frozen Coke."

Ripped shirt? That got me off the bench. My favorite thing in the world, my vintage Ramones T-shirt, had a three-inch tear right across the logo. I let out a string of curse words that caused a cop to come over and tell me to shut up.

"I loved this shirt!" I said out loud to no one in particular.

"Well," my cellmate replied, "then stay away from those frozen Cokes. They've been known to rip clothes and pop you in the face a couple of times."

He was fast with that one, a real wise guy. I wasn't in the mood to laugh, but I liked his attitude.

"What's your name?" I asked him.

"Nate. Yours?"

"Connor."

He shifted around and sat hunched over facing me. "Well, Connor," he prompted in a lower voice so no one else could hear, "tell me what happened to your face."

"I got suspended this morning for fighting with a guy at school."

"You go to Edgemont?"

"Yeah," I said, "but I'm on vacation right now."

"Yeah?" Nate said, "I thought I'd seen you before. No offense, but your hair stands out."

I nodded. "Are you a senior?"

"Yeah," he said, "but I'm on vacation, too. So tell me how this frozen Coke messed you up."

So I told him about the school fight, my jerk boss, the parking lot fight, and the robbery. How could this much junk happen to one guy in one day? It was like a convoy of manure trucks were lined up, and I was the dump site.

"If you ask me," Nate added when I had brought

him up to date, "your boss, what's his name?"

"Ken."

"Ken's the one you needed to punch."

"Yeah, that's what I'm sayin'!" I was sitting up by this time. There wasn't much ice left in the napkin. I mostly held a semi-cold napkin that was dripping on my clothes. It made me look like I had bladder-control problems. "All I wanted to do was do something useful with my time off."

I looked around the cell. "I'd say this is the exact opposite of what I had in mind." I looked at Nate. "So, why are you here?

"Well, I was buying this frozen Coke . . . ," he started.

I smiled a little, but my face hurt.

"I stole a car," he said. "Three days ago, I woke up and decided it was time for a road trip. I went down a street, found an unlocked car with keys, and took off. I love the open road."

"How'd you get caught?"

"Speeding," he said. "Doing 90 in a 35 zone."

"Are you going to fight it?"

"Not too much to fight," Nate said without even a blink. It was as if his fate was decided, and that's all there was to it. "The police cars have video recorders. They've got me speeding and getting out of the driver's seat."

"They tell me I'm on video too," I said. "But that's impossible, since I didn't actually do it!"

"Yeah, right," Nate mumbled. "That's what you keep saying."

Somebody banged on the bars of the cell. It was Chicken Lips.

"Your dad's here."

That was my biggest shock of the day. "Really?"

Chicken Lips didn't answer. He just opened my cage and jerked his thumb toward the door.

CHAPTER FOUR

Caught on Tape

Chicken Lips said nothing to me all the way down the hall. He stopped at a door, pushed it open, and waved me inside. Then he left. That's really all I wanted him to do in the first place.

The room was gray and bare. There was a table, four chairs and a TV on a rolling cart that made me think of school. Hmmm. School is like jail? I'd had that thought before.

On one side of the room sat Dad. He nearly blended in with the gray gloom of the walls. He

slumped in his chair as if someone had just picked him up like a pile of dirty clothes and plopped him into the metal chair. Looking at the two of us, you'd think he was the one in jail instead of me.

I tried to give him a little credit. This was the second time today he had left work to get me out of trouble. The police station was a little worse than the principal's office though. Maybe he was stepping up to be the father he should have been all along. Then I looked at his slump, and I knew he wasn't. Same old guy.

His heart wasn't into being here with me. He had no heart left. Mom had ripped that out years ago.

I stood there for a full minute, and Dad still didn't look up at me. His head hung low, his eyes toward the floor.

I grabbed the back of the chair across from him. I was hoping he would notice the blood caked on my knuckles and say something — anything — to me.

He didn't.

I plopped myself down in the chair as loud as I could.

He didn't move.

All right then. It was time to be direct. "Thanks for coming, Dad," I said. "Can we go home now?"

His voice came out of his mouth like a breeze from a tomb. "What did you do this time, Connor?" He still stared lifelessly at the floor.

"What did *I* do?" I shoved my chair away from the table. No way! He actually believed I robbed that store! Didn't he know me better than that?

"What are you talking about?" I yelled. "I was just trying to get a frozen Coke. I actually tried to catch the jerk who robbed the store! And they arrested *me*!" I started pacing. I had to get some of my anger out or I really would punch something.

"Connor," Dad's hollow voice echoed off the empty gray walls. "Was this just one more way to get back at me?"

I stared at him in shock. I moved my lips. But it took a few seconds for sound to come out. When the words finally came, they were loud. "What are you talking about?"

"This sets a new record, Connor. You've been suspended and arrested in the same day," he said. Finally he glanced up at me. I saw his face twist in shock as he looked at my beaten face, my ripped shirt and my blood–crusted hands. His jaw opened for a minute, and I thought he was going to cry.

But I was wrong.

"Oh my God! Look at you!" He was angry now. "When I dropped you at the house a couple hours ago after your *other* fight, you had a bruised eye! That was all!" He shook his head. "What are you doing to yourself?"

"Dad, I didn't do this to myself!"

"Yeah, you did!" He started waving his hands wildly. "You make yourself a freak, a target, and then you start fights. It's like you want people to take shots at you! You need to wise up!"

"Dad, don't start! It's too late for —"

He cut me off. "In September, you dyed your hair

neon red. You got in a fight. Two months ago, you pierced your ears. You got in a fight. Last week you put that rod in your eyebrow. But no fight. You must've been disappointed, 'cause today, you put on eyeliner. Eyeliner! And surprise. Surprise. You got in a fight at school! And I guess that fight wasn't enough, because there must have been another one! Do you like getting beat up? You want people to hate you?"

I could feel some of his angry spit coating my face. I didn't give him the satisfaction of wiping it off.

"Hey!" I poked at the air trying to pretend it was something to punch. "I told you before, Shawn started that fight this morning! He started talking about Mom and how many boyfriends she had. So I popped him!"

"Connor," his voice was a little quieter now. He didn't like to talk about Mom. We *never* talked about Mom. "I don't care about Shawn. I don't care about this morning. Just tell me, why are you in jail?"

"I went to the pizza shop to see if Ken would put me on the schedule this week."

"I told you not to leave the house!"

"You want me to just sit on my butt and watch TV for ten days?"

"You wouldn't be here right now if you did! It's your attitude, Connor. Somehow, you've got to fix that attitude."

"Do you want to hear my story or not?"

He waved me on.

"So that loser Ken, he tells me he'll think about it and talk to me in a week! In a week, I'll be back at school! One of these days, I'm gonna . . . "

Dad stared at me coldly. I might as well have been talking to the table.

"Then I'm pedaling home, and Shawn hits me with a rock. I'm not gonna let that go!"

"Connor, what about the store?" Dad blurted. "I've seen the video. You look like you're attacking the sales clerk."

"No, I was buying a drink, and I dropped it!" I

yelled. "Why don't you try to take my side for once?"

We stared at each other in silence. Then the door opened and some middle-aged guy with a striped shirt and bad tie came in. He had a folder and a video tape in one hand, a cup of coffee in the other. He was the spitting image of Mr. Donkas at school.

The guy plopped the folder and tape on the table, but held on to that cup of coffee. "I hate to break up this family reunion, but we need to talk."

"Who are you?" my dad asked.

"Det. Sgt. Nelson," the guy snapped, flipping open a badge. Then he slid the tape into the VCR and hit play.

"Connor, I'm going to get right to it." The cop pointed at me on the screen walking up to the store counter. "We've got the whole thing on tape. Right here, you're approaching the counter." He pointed at the other guy walking around the store. "Here's your buddy in the black hoodie and sunglasses casing the place. And when he gets right here, you jump across the counter and attack the clerk."

I was amazed at what I saw. From that camera angle, I couldn't see my frozen Coke. It really looked like I was jumping across the counter at Riley.

"So, Connor," the cop said, pausing to gulp his coffee. "Who's your buddy?"

"I didn't —"

"Save it!" he cut me off. "Here's your buddy hitting Riley. And here's you attacking across the counter."

"I was just . . ."

"And here's your buddy leaving you. Now you're trying to catch up with him."

I saw myself run out of the store following the creep who hit had Riley.

This sucked. The video made me look guilty. It was so bad it almost convinced *me* I was guilty. I only had one defence left.

"Dad, you know I wouldn't do anything like this."

He shook his head. "I can't believe you'd go this far." He was looking at the floor again. That hollow sound was back in his voice. "The hair, eyeliner, fights . . . I knew you were just acting out because your mom walked out." His head shook and his arms were crossed. "I thought you'd get over it." He was shutting down like he always did when we started to talk about important things. "I never thought you'd go this far."

"Dad, I didn't do this."

My father said nothing.

The policeman with the bad tie spoke instead. "Connor, Riley is in serious condition. You already have robbery and assault charges. If he dies, you're looking at murder. Who is your buddy? Help us out, and we'll talk about lessening your charges. If not, and Riley dies, you're going to be tried as an adult." He tapped the TV screen. "The video doesn't lie, son."

It was like someone just rammed a vacuum cleaner nozzle right down my throat and sucked the breath out of me. Assault? Robbery? Murder? *Me*?

I managed to get enough air to say, "Dad?"

Head still down, arms still crossed, Dad said nothing.

This was unbelievable. I needed time to think. I needed a shower and some sleep. I needed to get out of here and get my thoughts together. I needed some help before my mouth got me in any more trouble. "Do I get a lawyer? Can I get bail? Do I get to go home until the trial?"

The cop was silent and Dad didn't move. At last, my father spoke to me. "I'm not going to baby you, Connor. You think you're a man? Then you take what's coming like a man. You can sit right here in a cell and think about what you've done." Without looking at me, he stood and walked out the door.

The cop with the bad tie slurped his coffee. Then he waved for Chicken Lips to take me back to my cell.

CHAPTER FIVE

Back in the Cage

"Hey, you're back."

Well, at least Nate was glad to see me. I tried to smile as I walked back to my bench, but I just didn't have it in me.

I could swear the bench was colder and harder than when I left. But I knew, as I lay there, that the only things colder and harder were my feelings for my dad.

"He's just going to let me rot here!" I said, mostly to myself.

Of course, talking to yourself when someone else is in the room isn't really talking to yourself.

"Who?" said Nate, startling me.

"My dad!" I yelled, as if Nate should've figured that one out. "Well, I've gotten this far without him, why would I need him now." I looked at the thick bars that formed the cage around me. "Yeah, I've come *this far* without him."

I lay on my back and shut my eyes. I just wanted to sleep and escape this whole mess.

But Nate was still bored and wanted the details. "So, tell me what happened."

I did. Lying there with my eyes shut, I told him every detail. "*I* would almost believe I was guilty from looking at that tape! Dad certainly did. What kind of father is that? Real fathers don't think their kids are guilty . . . ever. It's his job to believe in me when no one else does." I took a breath. "It's his job," I repeated.

I felt so helpless right then I wanted to cry. But there are a few places that crying could get you killed. One is during a math exam, and another is in jail with other guys who've done God-knows-what.

Nate gave me a couple of minutes to get myself together.

"Look, man," he said at last. "I've been through this whole thing a few times. Here's what's next. In a couple of hours, they'll find some lawyer for you. Then they'll take you before a judge, and you'll plead not guilty." Nate spoke like a tour guide, pointing out the sights. "And then, if you're really lucky, they'll give you some clean clothes, since you have blood all over those. Blood kind of makes people nervous. They'll put you in a different cell and keep you there for a couple of days until your hearing."

"A couple of days?" I'd only been here a couple of hours. I couldn't imagine being here a couple of days.

"Parsons!" Chicken Lips almost startled me off the bench.

Nate turned his head.

"Let's go." Chicken Lips opened the cell door and motioned Nate out.

Nate turned my way just before walking through the gate. "See ya, Connor. Good luck. And watch out for those frozen Cokes."

"Yeah, you too."

For the next few hours, I got to know the cell pretty well. I counted the bars (25, by the way). I studied the cracks on the cement floor looking for patterns (they all just looked like little rivers to me). I had just started counting the concrete blocks in the wall when I heard keys in the door.

Outside was a guy with dark brown hair and an old brown striped suit. He was standing next to a policeman I hadn't seen before. The guy scratched his head and walked into the cell.

"Hi, I'm Mr. Dennis." He put out his hand for a shake. "I'm your lawyer."

"Hi, I'm Mr. Connor," I said accepting his hand.

"I'm your jailbird."

He didn't smile. "Dennis is my last name. Patrick Dennis."

"Oh, sorry. I thought we were doing first names like in preschool."

Still no smile. I was feeling a little goofy after being cooped up in this cell alone for a couple of hours. That's why I made the cheap joke about his name. Patrick Dennis wasn't amused.

"Okay, if you'll come with me," he said with all the personality of a soggy sandwich, "I need to talk to you in private about your plea and the trial."

He took me back to the gray room and explained a lot of things about my rights as a minor and stuff. I've got to admit, I didn't pay a lot of attention. Instead, I was watching how often he fixed his hair and pushed up his glasses. I was listening to the insane number of times he said "okay" and "um," nearly every other word. Maybe he'd had a long day and his brain was fried. I knew how he felt.

He asked the guard for some wet paper towels

and an ice pack, so I could clean up for the judge. I was going to court in half an hour. There was no mirror, so I did the best I could to fix myself up while he talked.

"Okay. Let's start at the beginning," he said.

For like the eightieth time that day, I told my story.

"Wow, you've had a busy day," was his brilliant comment at the end. "Okay, then, um, I need to ask you about parts of the day to, um, get a good feel for defending you, okay?"

I nodded.

"The reason, um, you didn't go right home after your second fight with Shawn was . . ."

"I wanted something to drink and something cold to put on my eye."

"Um, you couldn't do that at home?"

"No!" I said probably too loudly, "because Shawn was going that way, and I didn't want to talk to him." Didn't he get this the first time I told him? And didn't he think I'd been asking myself that for hours?

"Um, don't you think you should have gone home instead of letting this kid . . . " he checked his notes, "um, Shawn, um, control where you went?"

"What?" I was shocked. "Why don't you stop lecturing me and help me! Do your job!" I wanted to sock him. But it's never a good idea to hit your lawyer.

"Okay, well, I'm looking at you," he said scratching his head. "And I see red hair and some places under the bruises that used to be pierced."

"So?"

"Do you look like this to be different? Or do you do this to be like your friends?"

"I don't follow nobody! What's your problem? Why don't we talk about getting me out of here?"

"Okay, I'm not trying to pull your chain. I'm just trying to understand the whole picture so I can represent you better."

"Well, stop trying to act like a counselor and be a lawyer!"

Mr. Dennis pushed up the glasses that didn't need pushing up. He scratched his head. He let out a deep breath and said, "Okay, Connor, here's the thing." He used both hands to make sure his glasses sat just right on his ears. "The police have a video of you attacking a store clerk and . . . "

"That figures!" I interrupted. "You think I'm guilty too! How am I supposed to prove that I'm innocent if my own lawyer thinks I should be in jail?"

He didn't answer for a long time. He seemed to be asking himself the same question.

Finally he spoke. "If you would let me finish, please."

"Go ahead then."

"Okay. Since the police have a tape that *looks* like it shows you attacking the clerk, and Mr. Riley has already told the police you were one of the robbers . . . "

I started to interrupt again, But Mr. Dennis gave me that warning pointer finger that all adults seem to have.

" . . . then, um, we have to find out how to prove a victim and a video are both wrong. Therefore, I need to go through this with you . . . in detail." He looked at his watch. "And it would be nice if we could do this in the next ten minutes, since we are expected to be in court in twenty."

"What do you need to know?"

"You fought Shawn for the second time. You decided to pedal to the store." There were no questions, so I just let him recap my mistakes of the day. There were a lot of them.

Mr. Dennis stared at my face. "Do you wear a helmet when you ride?"

"No." I could feel another lecture brewing, and I was ready to snap.

"Your eyes were nearly swollen shut from both fights."

"Yes. Yes." There were two fights. We've covered this! I wanted to scream.

"Why did you ride your bike when you had two swollen eyes?"

"Oh my God! Why don't you get out of my face and try to help me!" I stood up and started to pace. This guy was really getting on my nerves!

It was his turn to snap. "Because, if you'd shut up and stop fighting me for a minute, you'd see that this makes no sense!" he yelled. "Why would a kid with two swollen eyes, cut and bleeding, drive a bike to a corner store, lock up the bike and then try to rob the clerk?"

"Huh?" Now I sounded stupid.

"Think about it. It makes no sense!" Mr. Dennis was excited now, no longer angry. "The lock alone would prevent a quick get away."

"Yeah, that's right."

"And as far as having a partner with a car? That's nuts. I admit you have made some bonehead decisions today, but even *you* wouldn't let a buddy escape in a car while you were left with a locked up bike. You'd never let anyone take advantage of you like that! You'd punch him out first."

I think I should have been insulted by most of

what he said, but instead I said, "Wow! Mr. Dennis. You *do* understand me!"

"Anyone with any common sense can see that you wouldn't have anything to do with this robbery."

"Yeah, but do you think the judge will have any common sense?"

CHAPTER SIX

The judge did. I was out of jail an hour later.

Of course, that hour was kind of hectic. Still clutching his coffee cup like I might try to take it, the policeman in the striped shirt asked me a lot of questions. Since I was no longer a suspect, I told him what I knew. Sadly, that wasn't much. The only new information I was able to give was that the robber drove a dark green car, an older Honda, Toyota, Mazda, or something.

I thanked Mr. Dennis. There was a lot of typing,

stamping, and a little lecturing — something about staying home for the rest of my suspension. I tuned out that last part.

Since I'm a minor (and they reminded me of that twenty times), the police would only let me out if my dad picked me up. Then came the big surprise. Dad was able to tear himself away from the TV long enough to drive to the station.

If I measured the distance from the police station to the store where my bike was, and then back to our house, it would be only ten minutes. But that ten-minute car ride felt like the longest one in my life.

Dad only broke the silence once. "Sorry."

"You should've trusted me."

That was it. I didn't have anything else to say. I guess he didn't either.

When I had taken my bike out of the car and put it in the garage, Dad was already sitting in front of the TV with a cold beer in his hand. Nothing had changed for him. His life was back to normal.

On the other hand, I had just had the suckiest day of my life. Also I was still ticked that someone had let me take the fall for robbing that store.

I took a moment to mourn my ripped Ramones T-shirt. Then I took a shower to get the smell of the jail off of me. But the cleaner I got, the madder I became.

That robber hit old Riley and left me to take the blame.

I wanted — no — *needed* to go out and find that loser. I had no idea how I'd do it, but I had to get started right away.

However, I made the mistake of sitting on my bed for just a minute . . .

Thump. Thump. Thump. Thump!

I woke up to some music playing in my head. Normally, that would be okay, but I hated this song. The thing had no words and no real guitars. It was a heavy-bass song played with some kind of computer. It repeated the same beat forever. And it was stuck in my head. No wonder I woke up.

I opened my eyes to see a daylight-brightened room. A quick look at my watch told me it was 11:17 a.m. I was late for school.

I jumped off the bed and realized two things. First: I wasn't late. I still had nine days of vacation left. Second: I was wearing only a towel. I had fallen asleep right after the shower.

I put on clean jeans and my second-favorite T-shirt, the Dead Kennedys. That stupid thumping song was still playing in my head. I didn't know what it was, but it was getting on my nerves. So I went into the living room and turned the TV on really loud to drown it out. Some women were screaming at each other on a reality show. Perfect.

I grabbed some ice cubes and put them into a plastic bag. I grabbed half a bag of chips from the nearly empty pantry and planted myself on the couch. I balanced my head against a pillow so the ice would rest on my eye without me having to hold

it. I needed one hand to stuff chips into my mouth and the other for the remote.

Thump! Thump! Thump! Thump! That song in my head got louder. I turned up the TV, but it was no use. The thump was haunting me.

I turned off the TV, chugged some milk out of the jug and hopped on my bike. I had to get out of the house. I really needed to get out of my head.

I headed south down Bendigo Street, away from school, away from the police and definitely away from the corner store. I looked across the parking lots and could see a small figure tossing rocks at the night club walls. Shawn needed to get a hobby.

Like most things I do, I didn't really think about why I wanted to drive across the grass and parking lot toward the night club. I just did it.

"You know," I said, in my usual smart alecky voice, "if you're actually trying to break one of those windows, you've got lousy aim."

Shawn's arm paused for a second. Then he let that rock go. It made a faint whistle through the air until it cracked against the cement wall.

He picked up another rock and kept his eyes on the cinder block target. "I'm not going to fight you today," he said. I could tell he had a little trouble saying his T's.

He turned briefly, and I could see that he had some kind of retainer in his mouth. I guess I did hit his teeth after all.

I felt a little guilty about that, but I wasn't about to apologize. "Look, I didn't come here to fight either. I just needed to get out of the house."

Shawn tossed another whistling rock at the wall.

"You know, you can really throw," I said. I impressed myself. It wasn't often I said anything like that. "I remember when you were the all-star pitcher when we were little. Why don't you play anymore?"

He threw another rock. "I flunked off the team."

"That's a shame."

He turned toward me. "Are you being a wise guy again?"

"No, I mean it," I defended. "You've got a great arm. You should still play ball."

"Well, thanks." He threw another rock.

"Okay, then," I said after watching a few more throws, "I'm gonna go find something else to do." I aimed my bike back toward Division Street.

I had barely put my foot on the pedal when Shawn stopped me.

"Hey, Connor."

"Yeah?"

"Why are you so touchy about your mom?"

Right then, you could've knocked me over with a toothpick.

"What?" I wanted to make sure I had heard him right, but I knew I had. "Nobody likes it when you talk about their mom."

"Yeah, but usually the kid just yells at me, stares at me or puffs out his chest and acts all big and bad." Shawn mimicked the tough-guy walk most kids do before they fight. It was a little funny because Shawn still couldn't say all those T's, so he sounded like a real dweeb. I couldn't laugh though. I knew my beaten face made me look like a mutant.

Suddenly, Shawn's acting stopped. "I was only joking, man. And you flew into me as soon as the words left my mouth."

Yeah, part of me wanted to slug him again for bringing it up again. But I looked at his retainer. I figured he had earned a solid answer.

"Mom left us about a year ago," I blurted out. "She had been seeing other guys for a year or two before that I guess. I didn't know it at the time. Dad did." I stopped to take a big breath.

Shawn didn't interrupt.

"I was kind of numb at first, but Dad took it hard. He hates his job, hates the pay. And he's not too crazy about me."

Shawn was being patient, but I could see he wanted me to get to the point.

"Anyway, here's Dad's life: he comes home from work, grabs a beer and sits in front of the TV until he goes to sleep. I guess it drove Mom crazy," I paused for another breath, "then I guess it drove her away." I was looking down at the asphalt now. "I guess she couldn't find anything in that house worth staying for, including me."

For a moment, the only sound was a passing car on the road behind me.

I took a deep breath and put my game face on again. "So hey, that's it. Nothing more to say on all that crap."

Shawn managed a twisted comforting smile; his mouth must've really hurt. "Man, at least your parents aren't screaming at each other. Mine are at each other from the second they wake up until . . . I don't know when. I have to put on headphones to drown them out so I can sleep."

"Is that why you're out here?"

"Yeah," Shawn said. "If I'm lucky and neither one of them is home, they actually call me just to yell. That's why I don't have a cell phone. If they can't find me, they can't yell at me."

"That's a good idea," I assured him.

Have you ever had one of those moments when you run out of things to talk about? Then there's really nothing much else to do but look around and eventually say . . .

"Okay, then," I said. "I'm outta here. Have fun with your rocks."

"Yeah." Shawn picked up a chunk of concrete and prepared to fling it against the wall.

"Hey, Shawn."

"Yeah?'

"Do you ever get one of those songs stuck in your head, and it just won't leave?"

"Yeah, I hate that!" he yelled. "Like the worst are those commercial jingles. They just get in your head and rattle around all day."

"Yeah, well I've got some techno-thump song repeating in my head. It even woke me up this morning." I performed my best imitation of the song in my head.

"I can't help you there." Shawn gave me a surprised look. "That's not the kind of music I listen to. And actually, I can't think of anyone who does listen to that. Where did you pick that one up?"

That was a good question. I should have asked myself that earlier. So I thought about the rapid-fire thumping in my head. And I tried to use my addled brain to trace it back. Where could I have heard it?

Suddenly, my head cleared. "I heard it right before the robbery yesterday!"

Shawn turned. I had his attention again. "What robbery?"

"Aw, man, do I have a story for you!"

CHAPTER SEVEN

The Hunt

"And you didn't get a look at the guy?" Shawn asked for the third time. We pedaled toward the mall.

"No!" I yelled. "Some jerk punched me in the eyes, remember? It was a little hard to see much of anything!"

Shawn flashed a huge smile. I hoped it hurt.

Shawn offered to ride around with me while I looked for the robber. He said it was because he was bored with throwing rocks. But I think it was because we understood each other a little better.

Everybody has things that eat them alive. I was glad he was helping me get over mine.

"So," he yelled so I could hear over the cars and the wind. "You think this guy at the music store can really help you?"

"He should!" I yelled back. "I've bought a lot of disks from his store, so he ought to talk to me. Besides, there aren't too many people around here who listen to techno. And there aren't any other music stores in the Edge. If the guy lives around here, he has to buy his music at the mall."

"You know, Connor, there is this new thing . . . it's called the In-ter-net!" Shawn yelled.

"Yeah, well, the guy robs corner stores. I get the idea he's not too high-tech!"

A few minutes later we were walking through the mall. I wanted to stop by the pizza shop long enough to chunk a salt shaker at Ken, but Shawn hit me on the shoulder.

"Hey, did you see the robber's sunglasses on that video?"

"Uh, yeah."

"Well? What'd they look like?"

I thought for a minute. "I think they were your basic wrap-around glasses. They looked kind of like Oakleys," I said, "but I couldn't see a logo. So I guess they could have been knock-offs. I'd really need another look at the video to be sure. Why?"

Shawn pointed to the sunglass kiosk about twenty feet away from us.

"If he wore fakes, then I think your robber shops at this mall."

We both spun around in hopes of spotting the robber. Of course, neither of us knew exactly what he looked like. We must've looked pretty dorky spinning together like that.

"Hey, let's get to the music store," I suggested.

Sound Gallery had a good range of music. It had a lot of trendy pop music that I don't go for. But it also had a lot of 70s punk music on CD, which isn't very easy to find. With school in session for another two hours, the store only had one other customer.

That would make it easier to find what we wanted.

"Connor!" yelled a voice from across the aisles of CDs.

"Hey, Tyler, What's up?" My luck seemed to be getting better. Tyler had been in a couple of my classes at Edgemont, before he dropped out. Now he was working full time at Sound Gallery.

"Dude, are you skipping?" he asked. Then he got a little closer. "Aw, man, what did you do to your face?"

I pointed accusingly to Shawn, who didn't look any better than I did.

Tyler looked from one of us to the other. His eyes finally settled back on me. "I'm sure there's a story here."

"There is," I said, "but I was hoping you could help me with something before I get into all that."

"Sure, what?"

"I need to know what kind of techno music you have."

"Techno? You, Connor?" Tyler laughed. "What

do you want with that? I thought you were Mr. Punk Rock! Aren't you trying to start a band? Murder Monkeys or something?"

"It's Homicidal SWAT Monkeys. But this is for something different. We're doing research. And we need to see your techno stuff."

"Okay, down here we have Moby and there's more over here."

"Actually," I told him, "I'm looking for something a little different." I tried to hum and beat-box the thumping song in my head. I know it wasn't too good. I had only heard it through closed car windows. The sole other customer stopped to stare at me.

Tyler clapped when I had finished. "Very nice. Do you know 'Freebird'?"

I gave him the finger. "So, do you have anything that sounds like that?"

"The closest I have is some hardcore techno over here on vinyl." He led me to a really small section of records at the back of the store.

Tyler punched some buttons on one of the music sampling machines and gave me the headphones. Thump! Thump! Thump! Thump! It wasn't the same song, but it was definitely the same style.

"YOU DON'T HAVE THIS ON CD?"

Tyler pointed at the headphones.

I took them off and lowered my voice. "Why don't you have this on CD?"

"It's hardcore techno," said Tyler, showing off his music knowledge. "Most guys buy these for parties. They use turntables to mix and scratch 'em. So they need records."

"Most guys?" I looked at the section that barely contained a dozen records. "There can't be that many people who buy them," I said. "One person could come in and clean out your stock."

"Actually, there's a few people who buy 'em," Tyler replied.

Shawn and I exchanged looks.

I asked first, "Are any of them tall guys about like this?" I raised and spread my hands to show the size of the robber I saw in the video.

Tyler said in a guarded tone, "Yeah, there's a guy like that, I guess."

Shawn jumped in before I could, "What's he look like?"

Tyler gave him a funny what's-it-to-you look. "If it's the guy I'm thinking of, he does the shaved-head thing. He wears black most of the time. You know . . . black T-shirts, boots, sometimes jackets. There's not much else I can say about him."

"You wouldn't have his name by any chance?"

Tyler just stared at me. I knew I was asking him to put his job on the line. I've got to admit, I didn't care. I wanted to find this shaved-head, old-man-beating, me-framing loser.

At last Tyler sighed. "I'm sorry, guys." From his cold eyes, I don't think he really was. I think he was about ready for Shawn and me to leave. "The guy always pays with cash."

I picked up an album by the corners and spun it between my fingers. There was no way companies were still making records. So these probably took some effort to keep in stock. "Do you special order records for him?"

"Connor, what's going on?" Tyler wanted to know. He took a step back and crossed his arms. He was just about done talking to us. "You guys sound like cops," he laughed. "You ought to know I can't tell you any more."

"Look," I said, "I spent most of yesterday in jail because some hardcore techno guy framed me for a robbery."

I looked at his face. Maybe he just didn't want to get involved. Maybe he thought I was blaming him. I don't know. He wasn't offering any more help.

I changed my tone to see if I could win him back. "Tyler, I just want to get a look at these people and see if one of them is the guy."

I waited for some response from Tyler. Nothing.

"All I'm asking is if you'd call me on my cell when he comes in."

Tyler looked at us. I could feel his eyes really

focusing on our swollen lips and bruised eyes. "If it's the guy I'm thinking of," he finally said, "he's gonna kick your butts!" He glanced around at the empty store. "All right, give me your number, and I'll call you if he comes again."

I wrote down my number and told him thanks. Then Shawn and I walked out of the store.

"He's not going to call you, Connor."

"Yeah, I know."

We walked a ways down the mall. We were stuck, and we both knew it. Finally, Shawn broke the silence.

"I'm thinking stakeout," Shawn suggested.

"Me too." It was getting easier to smile. For one thing, the swelling had mostly gone down. It just left behind those annoying yellow and black marks. For another thing, I finally had someone on my side.

CHAPTER EIGHT

Stakeout

On TV shows, stakeouts are so cool. There's a car. There's room in the back seat to take a snooze. There's always coffee and donuts. No one hassles the good guys while they sit there for days and watch. And at the end of, like, ten minutes, they always see the bad guy.

Let me tell ya, that's not the way it goes.

First of all — no car. Shawn and I had to hang around the mall. We weren't allowed to sleep on the benches. We had like nine bucks between us. So in the mall, that got us about one donut and water from the fountain. To keep from looking suspicious, we had to pretend to be shopping and still keep our eyes on the music store. After a while, mall security started following us around.

At ten o'clock, the gates started coming down in front of the stores. We called it a night. We agreed to take turns the next day. Shawn took the first watch in the morning, so I gave him my cell phone.

Day two of the stakeout was more of the same — no bald techno guy.

Day three was business as usual. I did have the added bonus of Ken coming out of the pizza shop to yell at me for loitering. I managed not to punch him. But it was really hard.

It's amazing how killing time can tire you out. I lay down around eight o'clock on the third day ready to catch some Z's when the house phone rang.

"Connor!" Dad shouted at me from his recliner. "Phone!"

Caller ID said it was me on the other end. That

meant Shawn was checking in.

"Hey, Shawn."

"Connor!" he said excitedly. "He's here! Get down here quick!"

I hung up, threw on some clothes and was out the door.

Dad hardly budged.

I was panting hard when I reached the mall a few minutes later. I tried to control my breathing, so I wouldn't attract too much attention.

Shawn stepped out of a cooking store and waved me over.

He pulled me quietly behind a dish display in the window. He pointed to the music store. "Look in the back," he whispered. "Is that him?"

I squinted. All I could see from this distance was a bald person in a black jacket. I couldn't tell anything else from this far away. It could have been my grandmother in a biker costume as far as I could tell.

"Aw, man, I don't know."

"He matches your description, and you can see he's shopping in the records," Shawn pointed out.

"How long has he been here?" I asked. "I mean there's only like twelve records. I figure there's not much to look at."

"He spent a while talking to Tyler."

"Really?" That news worried me. If Tyler was friends with this guy, I could be in some serious trouble.

"Yeah, they were talking and laughing," Shawn added. "I don't like it."

We watched for a couple more minutes and then a saleswoman came over. "Can I help you boys?"

"No, ma'am," Shawn said. He could turn on his polite switch when he needed. I should learn how to do that sometime.

She cut her eyes at us. "Well, you let me know if you have any questions. I'll be right over here." Her tone was a warning. We wouldn't be allowed to stay here much longer.

"How about if I go inside to look at some CDs so

I can get a good look at this guy?"

Shawn gave me a stupid look. "Connor, I hate to break this to you, but you have red hair and a beat-up face. There's no way he's not going to recognize you from a few days ago."

He was right, but I didn't tell him so. I just waited for bald techno guy to walk out. What could he be doing in the store this long? There were only a dozen records for crying out loud!

The saleswoman walked by us two more times. Finally, Shawn and I let out a sigh of relief. The bald guy took a record up to the counter. Tyler and bald guy smiled, exchanged cash, and talked briefly. Then bald guy walked out and passed right by our window.

"Well?" Shawn prompted.

"It could be him."

"Could?"

"Could," I said with attitude. "I couldn't see so well on Monday, remember?"

"Well, what do we do now?" Shawn returned the

attitude. "Did I just waste three days of my life for you to say 'could?'"

I thought for a second. "We follow him and see what kind of car he drives."

"Sounds like a plan."

We left our hiding place and took off. The bald guy wasn't too hard to follow. So we made sure we stayed twenty or thirty yards back. He was really cocky, I figured. He never turned around to look behind him or at any of the girls who were all over the mall by this time.

He turned and headed for an exit.

"Shawn, where is your bike?" I whispered.

"Down by the food court."

"How fast can you run?"

"I'll meet you near this door," he whispered. Then he sprinted down the hall. I didn't see any of the mall's finest chasing him. Then again, I wasn't watching him long. I was focused on the bald guy.

I tried to casually follow. Shawn's words echoed in my head: *You have red hair and a beat-up face.*

There's no way he's not going to recognize you.

I stayed to the side of the hall, not quite like a ninja, but close. Once outside, I was glad it was almost nine o'clock. I would be able to hide my red hair and bruises in the shadows.

Bald Guy, on the other hand, seemed to glow in the reflection of the street lights on his noggin.

I walked a lane over from where he walked and kept behind him. About the time I was wondering if he had walked to the mall, he turned in behind a white van. I crouched and ran on my toes to be as silent as I could. SUVs make great cover for stealth missions in a parking lot.

I stopped and peered around an SUV. Bald Guy sat in a car that was the right shape as the one at the corner store. But I couldn't tell the color until he came out from behind the shadow of the van.

He switched his headlights on and squealed out of the space.

It was a green Honda.

Yes! And this time I would get the license

number.

"Connor!"

I turned to see Shawn pedaling toward me. Then I spun my head back to the green Honda and cursed. I had missed the plate number again!

"Shawn, try to follow him. I'm going to get my bike."

Shawn took off. It was dark, it was stupid, but we were going to get this guy's plate number.

I ran and looked over my shoulder to keep my eye on Shawn. I trusted him to keep his eye on the car. Good thing it was a weeknight. Traffic wasn't as heavy as it would be on a weekend. Still, we were trying to follow a car by riding our bikes. This was going to be tough.

I reached my bike and unlocked it as fast as I could. I lost sight of Shawn. I didn't bother winding the cable lock back on my bike. No time.

I pedaled through parked cars and over some lawn. Nothing could stand between me and the mall exit.

When I hit the sidewalk on Pinecrest Street, I could see the outline of Shawn's bike on Division. Ignoring the angry horns, I cut across the street. I took a shortcut through the diner's parking lot. I could see Shawn a little better.

He was turning past the library on the road that goes by the pond. That wasn't good. There were no houses down that road, no street lights, and the speed limit was much higher. There was no way we would be able keep up. Once Bald Guy got down that road, he was history.

I turned the corner to see that Shawn had stopped. He was panting on the grass near the pond. He got off his bike when I pulled alongside him.

"I couldn't keep up," he apologized.

I hopped off and let my bike fall over. I was too tired to mess with the kickstand. "That's okay," I said between breaths. "You must've been hauling it to follow him this far."

"Yeah," he said with pride and obviously as

winded as I was. "But I did get part of his plate number: KMD." He paused to breathe. "There were three numbers, but I can't remember them." He took a breath. "I think there was a one, but I'm not sure. Sorry."

"Don't be!" I said. I was excited. "We've got a description of the guy and the car. We've got part of the license. Shawn, you're awesome! "

What wasn't awesome was the sound of the revving engine and the squeal of tires just a few feet behind us.

CHAPTER NINE

Going to Have Some Fun

At the sound, I dove into Shawn, knocking him down the slope toward the water. I rolled over and up in time to see the green Honda run over our bikes. The sound was horrible. There was a crunch followed by a noise like dragging a rake across a steel door.

The headlights flicked on, and the car spun around to shine on us. Bald Guy revved the engine.

"Don't move, Shawn," I said focusing only on the windshield. "He can't run over us here. He'll sink his car."

The engine revved again.

We stood a minute catching our breath.

I heard the triple click of the gears shifting into park. Bald Guy was going to get out, I figured.

I weighed our odds. He was much bigger than me, but there were two of us and only one of him. If Bald Guy got out of his car, Shawn and I had the advantage. I clenched my fists, ready for a fight. Out of the corner of my eye, I could see Shawn ready for the attack. Bald Guy was toast.

The door opened. It was hard to see much other than the headlights. I could see a boot hit the ground and a bald head shining in the moonlight. Then Bald Guy slammed his door and stepped into the light. In his hand I saw the billy club, a tonfa.

"You little boys should be home. It's a school night." He spun the club by the side handle. He knew how to use the thing.

For once, I had nothing clever to say. I tried to swallow the lump in my throat while stepping a

little way to my left. Shawn edged to his right. Divide-and-conquer was the unspoken plan. I looked at the club. Run-for-our-lives seemed like a smarter option.

I'd gotten Shawn into this mess, so I thought it was only right for me to draw Bald Guy's fire. That would give Shawn a chance to get away. He'd have to run on foot of course, since he'd need a spatula to get his bike off the grass.

I fake stepped toward the bald guy and quickly stepped back. Bald Guy lurched at me and swung. With my reflexes back to one hundred percent, I dodged the swing. Fast as I could, I rabbit punched him twice in the kidneys. At school, that would put most guys on the ground. But Bald Guy only flinched a little. Then he came back with a left-handed swing that I wasn't ready for.

The club caught me in the stomach. I went down hard, gasping for air.

I heard a thud and bald guy cussed. I can only assume that Shawn found something to throw and put his pitching skill to work.

I forced myself to my knees. Over beyond bald guy, Shawn reached down to grab something.

He never had a chance to throw it.

Bald Guy was too close to him. Shawn couldn't get off a good shot. Instead, he pivoted and ran away. Shawn had made it only a few steps when bald guy threw the club sideways. The tonfa wiped out Shawn's legs. There was the crunch of breaking bone, and then a grunt as Shawn fell.

Shawn was going down, but that gave me time. I forced myself to my feet and tried to get to the car.

I heard the sound of fist hitting body. Twice. Then the darkness was silent.

I had to get to the car. I had to get to the police. *Me of all people!* I had to get help from the police. I took a couple more steps toward the car. Then I knelt down and vomited in the grass.

A hand clutched the back of my neck and dragged me to my feet.

"You're an idiot, boy," Bald Guy growled. "You

think I couldn't see you watching me when I was in the music store?" He turned me to face him. I punched him with my left. It wasn't much of a punch. Bald Guy backhanded me and dropped me to the ground again.

"You've got bright red hair that glows like a neon sign, kid." He lifted me with his hands on each of my shoulders. I wouldn't be throwing any more punches. "You think I couldn't tell who you were? You think I couldn't tell what you wanted?"

I tried to kick him. He wrenched my shoulders to the side so hard I thought my back would snap. He banged me on the trunk of his car. I wanted to throw up again.

"You were better off in jail, little boy."

He opened up the back door and threw me inside. He stuffed my feet in and closed the door.

He sat in the driver's seat and put it in reverse. He backed over our bikes again just to be mean.

"You and me," he said, "we're gonna have some fun."

I lay on the seat curled up, feeling the worst I ever had in my life. I was in extreme pain. I was worried about what shape Shawn was in. I was scared about what was going to happen to me. Things were about as bad as they could get.

Then he turned on the techno.

CHAPTER TEN

Don't Get Fancy

I couldn't tell where we were going. The lights from the street pulsed waves of light through the car, not quite to the beat of the bass.

"Here's what we're going to do." He didn't yell. He didn't turn down the music. But I could hear every word he said.

He opened the glove box and took something out.

"We're going to go rob a store," he said. "And by 'we,' I mean 'you.'"

"You're out of your mind," I said, as tough as I could.

He laughed and parked the car. "Sit up."

The pain hurt so bad I almost screamed. Then I saw where we were.

We were parked in front of the big 24/7 store on Bendigo. "You're out of your mind!" I repeated it much louder this time.

Bald Guy laughed again and lifted a gun. He pulled the slide back to make sure it was loaded. He let it bang closed for effect.

"What I think," he said in a growl, "is that you are going to do whatever I tell you."

"You just hit Riley's place a few days ago," I protested. My voice felt stronger all the time. If I could stall just a few more minutes, maybe I could regain my strength enough to do something. "The cops will be watching all these stores now."

"Yeah, I thought of that," he said. The growl was gone and a smug smile sat on his lips. "That's why I wanted you here. You're like a bright red target that pulls every eye in your direction."

"This is stupid," I told him. "You'll be on tape again, and they'll nail you this time."

He smiled. "I'm not going in, kid. You'll be the guy on tape. And then you'll bring the money to me."

"I have to?"

"Yeah, kid. You have to."

"Okay," I said, pretending to go along. *Then I'm going out the back way, smart guy! You'll never see me again! Not until I've got every cop car in Edgemont down here.*

I grabbed the door handle, eager to get out of the car.

"Hold on," he yelled. "From here, I can see the clerk, the phone and you. If you don't rob this store, I'll shoot both of you. If you try to call the police, I'll shoot both of you. If you run away, I'll shoot the guy behind the counter . . . and you'll get blamed." He waved the gun for effect. "So don't get fancy, and don't try to do something smart. You've got three minutes. Got me?"

I nodded. So much for my big plans.

"I got you."

I stepped out of the car and walked slowly toward the store. My stomach was killing me and my mind was swirling. Whether I robbed this store or not, bald guy planned to kill me. It was as simple as that. Now what was I going to do?

I walked in and nodded to the clerk, a young kid, just a little older than me. I think I even knew him from school, some class or other. There was no way I'd let him get shot. I was already feeling guilty enough about Shawn.

The clerk's eyes followed my every move. I just knew Bald Guy was smirking in the car. My hair did attract attention.

"Can I help you with something?" the clerk said.

"Not yet," I replied.

I pretended to look at something in the chips aisle. Then I started to look for some kind of weapon to use against baldy.

No lighters, pocket knives, nail clippers, lighter fluid, pepper spray. Nothing. I glanced at the counter. He had all those items stashed on the wall out of the customers' reach.

I briefly thought of getting a frozen Coke and robbing this guy. That way, at least the clerk would stay alive even if I didn't.

Frozen Coke. What had Nate said in the holding cell? Watch out for those frozen Cokes. Then it hit me like a flash. *Good idea, Nate. Frozen Coke is a great idea.* I grabbed a random bottle of pop and headed to the candy aisle. I snatched what I needed and walked slowly toward the counter.

CHAPTER ELEVEN

Smile for the Camera

The clerk still had his eyes locked on me.

"Hey," I said keeping my calm pace. "Do NOT look out the front window."

I had to hand it to the kid; he didn't look. I would've looked.

He did glance under the counter. I figured that must be where he hid an alarm or some sort of weapon.

I reached the counter and slowly took out my empty wallet. "There's a guy with a gun in the car outside. You have some pepper spray or something?"

The clerk's eyes were shifting. I could tell he wanted to look outside. He didn't know whether to believe me or not. But he wanted to do something. He glanced under the counter again.

"I guess that's a no," I said unscrewing the cap quickly.

I handed the confused clerk a video rental card and hoped it looked like a credit card from behind a car windshield. While the clerk stared at me like I was crazy, I opened the pack of Menthos I had picked up a moment ago. My three minutes were up.

I heard the techno get louder. Bald Guy must be out of the car.

"If you have any kind of weapon behind the counter, get it now!" I shoved two Menthos tablets into the bottle and screwed the cap on a couple of turns. The chemical reaction started right away.

Bald Guy flung the door open raising his gun as he stepped in. I tossed the Coke bottle at him with all my might. The bottle hit him in the chest. The foam sprayed all over.

Exploding Coke doesn't stop bullets, and I didn't expect it to. But it did confuse bald guy for a few seconds, and that's all I needed.

I jumped over the counter and found a small baseball bat behind the counter. Then I rolled out of Bald Guy's line of sight, and clutched my stomach. The pain was almost unbearable.

Bald Guy fired once through the counter. He wasn't even close, so I knew he didn't know exactly where I was. The clerk was crawling away, past the cigarettes. I knew I had to act before bald guy found one of us.

The clerk's shoes made a sound against the floor. It was time to move.

I pulled the bat to my left as I stood up. Then I let bald guy have it. Since he was taller than me, I only hit him in the shoulder. It wasn't the head shot I would have liked, but it kept him from shooting the clerk. And from his grunt, I knew I had hurt him.

I wound to the right and caught him in the chest. Bald Guy moaned, and then he fell to the floor. I kicked the gun across the room.

I thought about hitting him one more time. It would have felt good. I would have squared us for the beating he gave me. But I didn't. He wasn't going anywhere. If he tried to stand, I'd clobber him.

I could hear the clerk talking on his cell phone. The cops would be here in a minute. And this time, I wasn't the one going for a ride.

As Bald Guy clutched his chest, I let myself laugh. "Smile pretty for the camera."

I got out of the hospital emergency room a couple of hours later with a bandaged rib. The police took my statement and sent me on my way.

Visiting hours at the hospital were long over, but a nurse let me go up and see Shawn. His head was all wrapped up. The nurse told me he was being treated for a concussion. He had blacked out by the pond and called 911 when he came to.

"Lucky thing you had my cell phone," I said.

"Yeah, lucky for you!" he shot back. His words were tough, but his voice was weak.

I nodded. He was right. The police showed up as fast as they did because of Shawn. There were cops out looking for the green Honda even before the clerk called.

"So how long are you here for?" I asked.

"Maybe tomorrow. They want to do some tests." His voice was a little weaker this time. "If they release me, I'm supposed to take it easy."

I nodded. I could tell he needed rest. "Okay, Dad's waiting for me in the car. He says he wants to talk." I smiled a little. *A real talk!*

"Your dad?"

I noddedd. "I'll stop by tomorrow."

Shawn nodded back. His eyes were nearly closed.

I turned to leave, but I had forgotten one thing. "Hey, Shawn."

"Huh?"

"Thanks." I opened the door to go.

"Hey, Connor."

"Yeah?'

"What are we going to do with the rest of our vacation?"

Check out these other EDGE novels

Behind the Door by Paul Kropp. Jamal and his buddies like to hang out in the basement of an old warehouse. Things are cool until a strange door appears on an inside wall. Of course, the guys have to look behind the door — and then the horror begins.

Dancing on the Edge by Sharon Jennings. When Bonnie-Lee crosses Division Street to go to the arts high school, she changes her name and her life. But she has to work hard and take some risks to win respect for her dancing.

Turf Wars by Alex Kropp. Kasim and his friends aren't much of a gang. They're not like Crips or Bloods, they're just a bunch of guys who hang togther. But that doesn't stop the Parkside Prep guys when they decide to clean up the Edge.

Tony Varrato is a high-school English language arts teacher and author. He has created teaching materials for Prestwick House and the State of Delaware Department of Education, but *Outrage* is his first published novel.

When Tony is not writing or grading papers, he's outside: running, kayaking, body boarding, biking, skiing and hiking. He lives in Delaware with his wife Bonnie, three kids (Dylan, Zack and Arina), three cats and one dog. For more information, see his website at www.tonyvarrato.com.

NO TEACHERS ALLOWED:
For online discussion of HIP Edge novels and characters, student readers are invited to the HIP Edge Café.
www.hip-edge-cafe.com

For more information on HIP novels:

High Interest Publishing – Publishers of H·I·P Books
407 Wellesley Street East • Toronto, Ontario M4X 1H5
www.hip-books.com